SNAPSHOTS

R.Healing

Important

Paperback: ISBN 978-1-7391320-0-2

Further contact details and information can be found at www.churchouseconsultants.com

SNAPSHOTS

The idea behind these snapshots was to stimulate the imagination - and have some amusement.

On the whole, each snapshot provides just a glimpse of a scene which I hope will lead the reader to a much broader and richer scenario. The snapshots have been deliberately left without a "proper" conclusion, much in the way that when looking through a photograph album of unknown people and scenes one can imagine what they might be or, possibly, what might have happened after the photo was taken.

It might be best to take one snapshot at a time to allow the mental picture to build up. I would recommend leaving a gap of several days between each one.

I do hope you enjoy them. Perhaps you might like to write your own?

Rosemary Healing

A small movement under the sheet, a breath,
and the eyes opened.

I woke with a thundering headache, stretched out, robot-like, for the aspirin, swallowed an indefinite number and looked out of the window.

It was autumn.

It may well have been autumn the previous day, but just then I was in no position to know. The sun was enjoying colouring the leaves in the latest autumnal range, and the leaves were showing off, gliding gently and untroubled to the ground.

I'm a writer, you see, and even with the hangover of the year I can't help thinking in well-turned phrases.

Fresh air, I thought: black coffee and fresh air.

I sat on the bench overlooking the tiny conservation area which serves as my garden and watched the autumn. Without my headache it could not be thought of as a sad season - there were too many radiant colours, wonderful contrasting effects and exotic arboreal skeletons strip-teasing their way through the few weeks before winter.

Another leaf thumped to the ground. (God, is this 'stream of consciousness'? I enquired. More like the stagnant weeds of …).

My headache was gradually pushing off to haunt some other unfortunate, so I addressed myself to a number of unanswered questions:

1. What day was it?
2. What was I supposed to be doing with it?
3. Why had I woken up? - I was going to say in a post rigor mortis state, but why had I woken up? was enough.

The questions remained unanswered as I pursued a second cup of coffee. The jar rolled under the table, and as I followed it the first coherent thought of the day struck me. At the same time the table struck my head as I misjudged my height.

The smell of drying salt, black seaweed draped over rocks, empty shells among the pebbles, grey clouds over grey water and the cliff looming threateningly over the bay.

Right, children, settle down. I don't mean under your desk, Tom.

Have you all got pencil and paper? Fiona, stop drawing on your paper. What are you drawing anyway? I don't think that's very nice.

Now, today is Thursday, so are you ready for your spelling test?

(... Oh, b...er, it's Wednesday isn't it. It's supposed to be maths or English or something.)

Well, children, today we are going to do something completely different.

Legs going round and round like a whirlygig.

Wind attacking me in the face.

Mouth dry – keep it shut.

At last, a downhill slope!

Now, let's see … I think I'll wear this green dress because he once said that green was his favourite colour. Now which shoes? I must be careful with my make-up. Foundation and powder, a little rouge, eyeliner (not too much), the eyebrows are OK. What about lipstick? I've loads to choose from … I think I'll go with this one - it's dark and sexy. Now I'm ready to go.

Oh! That's my phone …

Hailstones beating against the bedroom window
demanding entry:

bedclothes gently drawn up, warm and comforting.

He was sitting at his desk, re-reading the draft for his detective novel. The plot was progressing well, with the characters and motives gradually becoming clearer. "Like the layers of an onion" came to him. "I can't use that, it's such a cliché" he thought. Then, like a flash, "I've got it!".

A. Oh, hallo, B. Have you just been to the concert here?

B. Yes, I have. Will you join me for a drink?

A. Yes – I think I've got time before my train. What did you think of the performance?

B. The violinist was brilliant, wasn't he? But what annoyed me was the person coughing all the way through that quiet section. Why can't people control themselves, or go out of the hall if they can't stop coughing? I wanted to kill that person!

Here we are. What would you like?

A. Um, actually, I'm not feeling too good. I think perhaps I'd better not stay for a drink after all. Sorry! Hope to see you again soon...

It gets darker as you go down. The light isn't very good in the cellar. The steps are rickety – it really all needs an overhaul. There's a noise … it sounds as if something is moving…

My time has come.
I speak my last.
My days, in sum,
Are running fast.

Can I cope?
Do my best?
Grab some hope?
Past the test?

Tomorrow will be the moment.
I'll cast off all my life,
And, by the end of the day,
I'll have acquired a wife.

The last leaf fell from the apple tree today.

The grey skeletal branches hang over the damp grass waiting for renewal.

Deep in a muddy trench we await the bombardment. It is cold and gradually getting dark. We can't move anywhere because we are guarding the particular area we know they want to take. How do you fill your mind when you are in a position like this? You have to keep some concentration going in case you are taken by surprise. Thoughts of home or friends - some of whom are dead - do not help. You must think of something positive to help the time pass. What could it possibly be?

A. Oh, hello, love. How are you? Chilly this morning, isn't it?

B. Hello. Yes, I ….

A. I was just saying to Edna next door - you know Edna, don't you, love - she had her feet done last year - do you remember? - and she hasn't been the same since. Well, I was just saying to her - we met when we went outside to bring the milk in - we often do, you know - often get in the milk at the same time and have a little chat on the doorstep. Well, this morning I said "It's getting colder, isn't it, Edna".

B. "………"

A. Are you all right, love? You look as if you aren't quite all there.

B. Yes, I'm fine, thanks. Although …

A. You have to be ever so careful in your condition. My goodness me - I can remember everyone giving me advice when I was expecting Johnny. "Do this. Do that. Eat this. Don't eat that. Take these tablets. Don't take them tablets. Wrap up warm. Don't get too hot."

Mind you, the best thing I always say is to be sensible and do what you like.
Of course, you haven't really got anyone to give you advice, have you?

B. Well, no …

A. If there is anything you need - anything at all - you just let me know. (B. Thank you) No don't thank me. I'm not a bad cook, you know, and of course I've got a washing machine, and, believe it or not, I enjoy cleaning. I really like to see a room gleaming. I used to slave away to get the house clean for my Bert - not that he ever noticed, of course - clean or dirty, it was all the same to him.

B. It's very kind of you …

A. Don't think twice about it, dear. It'll be like looking after my own daughter and her little one. Now that Johnny's in Canada - I never did much care for that wife of his, you know, dear - and Elspeth's up in Aberdeen, I miss my grandchildren. When's your baby due, dear?

B. Not for another three months yet, but …

A.   Oh, that's nice - it'll be a summer baby. Johnny and Elspeth were both born in the autumn: Johnny on the 22nd of September and Elspeth on the 15th of October. A summer baby's so much easier. You can leave the pram outside - so much healthier. Of course, you can't leave the pram outside, can you, dear, being in those flats, but why not wheel it along the road and you can put it on my piece of grass and you and me can have a coffee and you can keep an eye on it the whole time. You hear such dreadful stories nowadays, you can't be too careful.

B.   I shall look forward to that.

A.   That's settled then. Don't you worry about a thing.

I must be getting along, dearie, and get my shopping done. I've got the old people's lunch to see to, and it's my afternoon for cleaning the church brasses.

Have you met the new vicar, dearie? He's ever so nice. Really one of the old school. None of your new-fangled guitars and dancing in the aisles. Good old-fashioned, God-fearing worship - and he's really pleased with all that the ladies do, cleaning and polishing and arranging the flowers. Do you go to church, dear? I haven't seen you there. I'm not

so sure about that Mrs. Vicar, though. Seems a snooty sort of woman to me, with her tweed skirts and pearls. I think he needs protecting from her. The ladies of the church take it in turns to help him, you know, so he always has someone to call on. I don't think she's as much use as she'd like everyone to think.

Still, mustn't be un-Christian must we, dear? Are you going on to the shops?

B.	No, I'm waiting for someone, actually.

A.	Well, I hope they come along soon. You can't afford to get cold in your condition. Whoever it is shouldn't make you wait like this - you'll catch your death. Better go, then, or I'll be late all day. Can I get you anything at the shops?

B.	No thank you.

A.	You know that supermarket may have "All You Need Under One Roof", but can you find it? Last week I spent ten minutes looking for tomato ketchup only to find it on top of the ice cream. I ask you, where's the sense in that? Still, I suppose it's easier being able to do your shopping all in one place.

Right, I'll love you and leave you, dear, and you look after yourself. It's chilly this morning, isn't it?

Do you know, I was just saying to Edna next door [fade] - you know Edna, don't you, love?

Dark trees silhouetted against a brilliant blue sky, spears of sun bursting through in between the branches.

The scent of moss, stretches of ferns, the humming of bees.

The usual smell of disinfectant. The now familiar trek through the corridors to the children's ward. The clutch at my heart as I walked though the door. I turned to his bed - and there he was, sitting up and smiling!

Hello.	Good afternoon.
Have you had a good day?	Not too bad, thank you.
What classes have you had?	Forms 4 and 5.
Do you teach X?	Yes, he's in form 4.
How do you find him?	He's fine in class but he doesn't mix much.
What about his family?	I don't know much about them,actually.

He wrote an essay. It struck me
as interesting. I've got a copy of it.

Here, have a look.	I see what you mean.

Now I read it again

- Oh my goodness!	I think we had better…

Yes!

A dark interior.

A faint smell of incense.

Flickering candles.

Silence. Peace.

The weeds grow thickly, smothering the soil.
Roots like tree trunks, impossible to dig.
The fork gets stuck and won't come out.
Is it worth this useless toil?

Maybe if I carry on
I might hit something buried there.
Gold or silver, I don't mind -
Something valuable and rare.

Get the fork out and have another go.
The thought of treasure makes me strong.
The weeds work hard to bar my way
But I'll be rich before too long!

Half a dozen people sitting in a circle in silence.

Prayer group?

Book club?

Mindfulness session?

No, doctor's waiting room.

I think everything's ready. We've got twelve people coming, so the table is fine. All the drinks are standing by and the food is ready in the kitchen.

There's the bell - they are beginning to arrive. How nice to see so many friends on such an occasion.

Everyone's here now so we'll serve the meal. Oh, the bell's gone again.

Shall I go and answer it?

Good evening. Oh Lord! It's you.
What are you doing here? Why have you come tonight?
What am I going to do?

Huge, excited crowds pushing forward, yelling in the oppressive heat.

The combined smell of human flesh, alcohol and beefburgers.

The group on stage starts up. Rapturous applause, then silence.

A. Hi!

B. Hi! come on in. Do you want to come upstairs?

A. Can we take some coffee with us? I'm dying.

B. Sure. Move, cat. I need to get to the kettle.

A. Hello, Smog. Aren't you gorgeous!

B. Like name, like brain. Here's your coffee.

A. Thanks.

B. Do you know what caffeine does to your system?
It contracts …

A. No, I don't want to know, thanks.
I can't live without it.

B. That's addiction, that is.

A. Yeah. Hey, did you watch that new comedy last night?

B. Mm. It was hilarious. My father poked his head round the door just when they were - you know …

A.   Yeah.

B.   He said, as he always does, "Why do these programmes always have to be so vulgar?"

A.   And you said, "This is the only rude bit in the whole thing and you had to come and see it."

B.   Right. You could tell he didn't believe me, though. He's sweet.

A.   Where are your parents, by the way?
   The house is very quiet.

B.   They've gone off to some holy-type meeting at the church. Very worthy stuff. Vicky is at a friend's and Tamsin is probably riding her bike round and round the block to annoy the old b----- who lives across the road.

A.   So if we hear crashes and screams -

B.   We'll go and scrape Mrs. Evans off the pavement. Hey, do you like my new lipstick?

A.   Mm. Can I try it? Does it stay on?

B.   Not when I'm with James!

A new pair of trousers was what I was after.

I had come alone, not requiring wifely comments.

I tried on several pairs, all with something wrong -

waist too tight, leg length too long or too short etc.

Looking at myself in the fitting room mirror,

I saw a foolish man trying to make a sensible
decision on his own.

Have you got 6 across?	No, haven't a clue.
Could it be an anagram?	I suppose so, but what of?
If we get 5 down that would give us another letter.	Go on, then.
Ah! Got it! It's an anagram of "oriental".	OK, so what is it?
I'm going to make a cup of tea. **........**	

A warm patch left on the cushion.

Soft footsteps heading for food.

What would you like me to do with your hair today?

Much the same as usual, I think, thank you.

It's grown a lot since I last saw you.

That's because it's been a while. I've been away.

Oh? Where did you go?

Only to Yorkshire, but the extraordinary thing is I met a woman who said she used to live here.

Really? That's strange isn't it? Could you just turn your head a little to the right? Did you get her name?

No, she was a bit odd so we just had a short conversation. I didn't take to her at all - she was very overweight, unattractive and full of herself.

Do you know, I think I know who you are talking about. Did she have dyed blond hair?

Yes, she did. It must be the same woman. Ow! Don't pull too hard.

Sorry. Is that better? You know what, that woman has a
very interesting history. She left here after something
terrible happened. I can't tell you about it because at the
time I was sworn to secrecy but I was partly involved.

Oh, do tell. It can't do any harm now.

Well… By the way, do you want the parting at the side
again?

They sat in what he thought of as companionable silence and she as dull intimacy.

The sun crashed scarlet though the stained glass window and the gargoyle on whose face it fell grinned wickedly.

Complete silence.

Not a rustle, not a snap, not the flap of a wing.

Bluebells filling the air with scent.

Lightning Source UK Ltd.
Milton Keynes UK
UKHW010958191222
414150UK00011B/1884

9 781739 132002